THE GUIDE TO THE FLYING ISLAND

To Heather — with every happy wish for you — always. Lee.

THE GUIDE TO THE FLYING ISLAND

a novella

Lee Upton

Edited by Joseph Bates

Miami University Press
Oxford, Ohio

©2009 by Lee Upton
Library of Congress Cataloging-in-Publication Data

Upton, Lee, 1953-
 The guide to the flying island : a novella / Lee Upton ;
edited by Joseph Bates.
     p. cm.
 ISBN 978-1-60743-571-6
1. Islands--Fiction. 2. Apparitions--Fiction. 3. Tour
guides (Persons)--Fiction. I. Bates, Joseph, Ph.D. II.
Title.
 PS3571.P46G85 2009
 813'.54--dc22
                                        2009005907

Printed on acid-free paper in the
United States of America.

Also by Lee Upton

Poetry:
The Invention of Kindness
No Mercy
Approximate Darling
Civilian Histories
Undid in the Land of Undone

Prose:
Jean Garrigue: A Poetics of Plenitude
*Obsession and Release: Rereading the Poetry of
    Louise Bogan*
*The Muse of Abandonment: Origin, Identity,
    Mastery in Five American Poets*
*Defensive Measures: The Poetry of Niedecker,
    Bishop, Glück, and Carson*

For Cecilia C. E. Ziolkowski

1

There were stories of Jesuits blown off-course, of early native peoples disembarking to bury their dead under basalt slabs, and of two Norwegian brothers creating a settlement, the latter a claim without any evidence other than local feeling. It was indisputable that there had been the beginnings of a monastery—a stone dwelling long ago reduced to a ruined foundation. In 1956 a rudimentary chapel was erected by men from Truror who claimed they found evidence that early inhabitants had managed not only their spiritual lives but storage shelters at the summit. Two decades later much of the island was purchased by a millionaire who, like many of his temperament, bought a thing so as no longer to have to think about it. The little concrete chapel, the three hundred steps leading to the summit, cut into rock and supported with crumbling cement, the tiny giftshop doubling as a tea shop, and at the lower elevation, the rim of cottages and bed and breakfasts on the south shore: all were given whimsical treatment in two guidebooks and a BBC program that spared the island a total of nearly seven minutes.

Before Jake Isinglass was farmed out to foster families, and long before he took boatloads of tourists to the islands, he was able to look out his bedroom window and study the distance to see if the island flew—an illusion much like that of clouds speeding across the moon. Better than watching the island was being at the island's summit, the ocean glittering far below like knives in a mammoth drawer. But Jake knew that with any boatload of religious people—for whom the island had become an especially popular destination—his joining them at the summit after he or his crewmate Kip gave their spiel about the island could be an imposition. He supposed, given his tendency to pant before the fiftieth step, he was a reminder of anything but lofty heights. Never mind. He liked to be alone, too.

The passengers on his boat that Friday were almost all women: glassy-eyed, every one of them wearing fringed bangs and weirdly high hair buns. Not Mennonites, but what were they? Their long skirts, like something from the prairie, a blue faded near-white and scuffed. The women clustered on the first couple of benches of his boat, and he caught a faint shuddering of lips from two of them. The men accompanying the women looked angry and aggressively modern. At least five of them were in leather jackets, which seemed unfair to the women, stuck in those funky prairie dresses.

His passengers didn't listen to Kip's lecture on the island's history but trudged past en masse up the path, speechless except for three of the men, mumbling and hanging together close as if blocking any other visitors.

Jake waited by the gift shop where the caretaker, Carlo, scrubbed off trestle tables. All around him light was breaking like a smashed mosaic. It took well over an hour before his passengers trickled down the cliffside, still bunched together as if roped. The group didn't visit the gift shop or stay for tea but clambered to the dock. By then the sky was growing steadily darker and Jake was looking forward to the return trip to Truror where the group filed off his boat into a waiting bus.

Only later when Jake took his skiff out that night and rounded the cove did he notice what was missing in the distance: the illuminated cross at the island's summit.

As soon as light allowed the next morning, Jake and Kip trudged up the three hundred steps and found burned candles first, then discovered mounded dirt where the cross was uprooted. A trench had been dug about six feet from where the cross should be. Jake tried to imagine the women carting off parts of the steel cross under their voluminous skirts. In the trench he began shoving aside clods of soil and small rocks. He endured a surge of nausea when he felt the strange softness.

The color came at him as he dug—a bright fleshy pink. His hands, burning up to the wrists, drove into the loosest soil. The kneecaps of his pants grew wet. He kept at it and then drew gently until out from the soil came what he feared was an entire baby, feather-light.

It was a baby's jacket, no baby. A tiny jacket that would fit a rabbit. Pockets in the jacket. The useless thought occurred to him: Why would a baby need pockets?

Jake turned to look up at Kip, who was standing there being unhelpful, but whose stunned eyes were blacker than ever. He went to work again, as if the little body was under the dirt and could be saved if he dug quickly enough. Kip knelt beside him and began digging too. Jake felt another grainy patch of softness—and then more. His fingers nudged at something fuzzy.

A little pink baby bonnet with feathery fake fur around it.

Kip found the shoes. Tiny white shoes smaller than his thumbs.

At the bottom of the first elevation, the two men discovered the cross leaning against the back wall of the chapel. It was a wonder that the caretaker hadn't seen it—that no one had discovered how the group moved the cross down the steps.

"Why do that?" Kip said. He and Jake were re-burying the baby's clothes at the summit. "I mean if you're going to bury a baby in effigy.… Wait. They didn't bury the clothes here and then throw the baby off one of the cliffs? They wouldn't do that, would they?"

No, Jake didn't think so.

"Shouldn't they have left some kind of marker about the baby?" Kip asked.

Jake reburied the shoes and jacket, tamping down the bonnet last.

He could imagine why it was that, many years ago, monks prostrated themselves at the summit, close to what they imagined as their God. He could understand that—the black nights, the winds whipping to drive off Satan and his wiles. But he could not understand why a baby's outfit would be buried on the island. He could not understand why anyone would want even the memory of a baby to be lodged in a place so motherless, with its steep vertigo-inducing cliffs and sharp clusters of rocks and lashing storms—unless you didn't think of your baby as a baby anymore but as some other force, cold and spacious and wide. You'd have to think your baby was steeper than the island.

With Kip he dragged the cross back up to the summit and remounted it in its socket. His hands on the heavy steel, the image of a crucified baby came to him. Those women—they must have imagined they carried the baby's spirit to the summit, offering that little soul up—why? So that it could expand and fill all of space? They had all been in on it, the whole group of them. A conspiracy. Well, if it rested their hearts...not that they seemed any more rested on the way back to Truror. Thinking back on it, he couldn't even tell which one had been the mother, all the women huddling, stone faced, turned away from him and Kip. The men on the other side of the boat had looked furiously detached, as if facing up to something they were regretting.

It wasn't exactly illegal, burying baby clothes. Taking down the cross—maybe that was vandalism?

Later that morning, while the island's caretaker was making tea for another tour group brought over by Doug Llewellyn's boat, Jake sat at the one trestle table that was outside the gift shop. He and Kip had gone back to Truror and picked up a boatload of tourists. There were only three couples, all now on their way up the summit. Normal-looking older people, for the most part. Jake could have gone to the summit with them, and they probably wouldn't have minded.

Clouds were massing gray to the west. A cold dash of rain landed on the knuckle of his right hand. He would like nothing better than to be back in Truror, making himself a sandwich before taking a nap without that poor baby or those women bobbing in his head and making him wince.

And then he knew what those poor weird people wanted for that baby.

The cross couldn't stand afterwards—after they labored to make themselves imagine what they wanted to imagine. Not after a resurrection.

2

There was a Catholic education conference in outer VanLieflin, and part of the group had made the
special effort to head for Truror. Jake was used to
nuns who dressed like dowdy businesswomen, or
those who wore a half-habit, their bangs showing
and their ankles exposed above their ugly shoes,
the kind that would never dissolve in a dump for a
million years. Shoes like block and tackle. Frankenstein shoes with Frankenstein stitches. But these
nuns were different.

He hadn't realized they made them like that
anymore. Retrograde nuns. A boatload of nuns in
full habit, black veils, little white placards on their
foreheads. Old-fashioned hard-liner nuns, white
women, faces dipped in flour, unreal, cakey. Plaster
nuns. A boatload of plastered nuns—that might be
interesting. But no: plaster nuns. The nuns lifted
their heavily shod feet whenever water slopped
across the floor of the boat.

Were they a half-cloistered sect, vowing silence?

Surely they didn't talk enough to seem normal.

He knew each was a separate human person, of course—though it would be impossible to feel those differences too sharply in a short boat ride—but he could tell that the nun with the deep wrinkles in her forehead held sway over the others, that when she shaded her eyes with her right hand the others felt a fluttering response. Judging by her moving but silent lips, one of the nuns was carrying on an old useless argument. A couple of nuns looked at him—he was sure—with disapproval. Not sniffing, but faintly disgusted. The legs of his shorts were too wide, maybe.

Out of the mist a mass of darkness reared, slabs of rocks with outcroppings and then, quick as two hands clapping, the island was wiped out again, and they were all staring though a gauze bandage.

The wind fanned out the nuns' black veils. He thought of crows bent over road kill, but then something didn't look right. A little nun on the third bench, alone. More cloth than body. As if she inherited her robe from an enormous nun. Or was a child playing dress up. When the boat took a swell he caught her looking his way. He couldn't read her expression—fear or exhilaration, her bony skull, the skin tight. Was she anorexic? Was that it? Was that why she was overwhelmed by her clothes? The incredible shrinking nun. Like an alien with her big, metallic-looking eyes. He knew then he would want to see what her face looked like when she reached the top of the island—if her face softened or grew more radiant.

Kip helped each of the nuns off the boat. A good kid. Hardly an ironic bone in his body. He liked nuns even if he was sure to be laughing at them as soon as they disembarked on the return trip to Truror. Kip disentangled the veil of a nun from a steel edging. Jake took his chance and reached out to help the nun in the too-big habit. Her hand was dry and small but wonderfully solid nonetheless. When she let go he could still feel the warmth of her palm. He felt a wave of self-repulsion. If this wasn't a sign of his going strange, what was? Nun flirting.

She glided, following the rest of the women several steps back from them. He didn't understand why she had chosen this cumbersome life for herself, which was probably as ill fitting as the habit she wore. On the path upward toward the chapel she hardly seemed sure-footed, tipping like a bell as she maneuvered.

When the nuns assembled in a circle, she kept at least five feet away, staring over Kip's head toward the summit. Jake crossed his arms as Kip began his speech, which amounted to a paraphrase from the most pretentious of the guidebooks. Kip was having fun in his own way. Although the words never seemed to fit his mouth, they appeared to impress the majority of visitors and amuse the rest.

In what year we can't know, the island began to gain its powerful pull. What we do know—incontrovert-

ibly—is that our sources are contaminated and rife with anachronisms. We can only bring to these imposing drop-offs some of our most imaginative speculations. What lived under the gaze of this stone bust? How have the winds whipped and shaped these once presumably recognizable forms into guardians of time?

We can ask certain questions. Monks of the distant past who devoted themselves to this island rock, who knelt to pray at the edges of these sheer vertical drops, what can we know of them and the arduous task of hauling water to the island, of keeping their foodstuffs on rocky land? For who is to say how the sublime is meant to expend itself on the eye? Surely, certainly— I'm quite serious—not I. So little to know, to be sure of, to secure an interpretation—.

Oh Kip.

The nun turned and leveled her eyes at Jake. The pure force of her gaze made him step back and blink as if her hand reached out and struck him. After she turned away, Jake studied the little nun's habit, wondering again if it were borrowed. He didn't understand the intricacy of these…these costumes. It occurred to him that if he walked at all quickly his right foot would land on her robes— and wouldn't that be awful, though the prospect of his coming so close to her, her pivoting and looking him full in the face again, that was something. Nerve-wracking to have those silvery eyes staring.

Even with her back turned he felt her presence, the air itself more granulated, and he was still considering what it would be like to see her face again when his boot caught at her trailing hem.

The cloth must have been dense as chain mail. She fell in a plop, a blob of cloth, the habit swarming over her.

He knew his face was flashing misery. Stepping on her like a big eighth grade kid playing a trick. *My little nun*, he thought. *Forgive me*.

After that he didn't go up to the summit with the nuns. What was the use? He might step on her on the way up and cause her to plummet backward down the steps.

He sat on a stone wall opposite the caretaker's cottage. Carlo's daughter was nowhere in sight, but she had tucked her bare-naked Barbies like plant stakes among the day lilies waving ahead of him in the thin soil of the cottage yard. The island was no place for a little girl unless she was playacting the 19th century and determined to admire the properties of lampblack. Jake could bet that living on the island had been an adventure for the caretaker—once—but the storms could wear out anyone's temper, and what nameless shrubs and dwarf pines that survived were gnarled twisty things, and for the most part the string of "charming" bed and breakfasts down by the pier, always with strangers packing in and packing up, couldn't offer much for a child.

The day was still crystalline with the taste of salt in it when the little girl came out of the cottage and began digging in the dirt.

Jake felt tightly aware of the suspicions that hover around a man alone with a child. He wondered why Carlo let her outside so easily, unattended. He kept the child in his peripheral vision—a little figure in a yellow dress working with a shovel nearly the same bright shade. She didn't seem aware of him, so busy was she burying one of her dolls up to the waist. Another doll was stepping off a garden stone, one leg balanced on the stone, the other tilted in mid-air.

When he looked toward the trail that led to the island's summit he saw no one. The pack of nuns must have rounded the bend. Soon a few of their number would creep down the cliffside, deterred from attempting the summit by vertigo or by the instability of the gravel, or made anxious by that stomach-dropping moment if one or another lost her footing. Those tourists—usually not the oldest, strangely enough—would mince their way down and have tea at the giftshop, giddy with relief and embarrassment.

After a while he realized that he hadn't been thinking but his mind had grown calm. The child was digging and talking to herself. Her little face was flushing pink as a peony in the heat but white around the nose and mouth. Her eyelids fluttered, and he saw she might be in the midst of a fever.

At last he couldn't help himself. "Shouldn't you get out of the sun?" he said. She squinted up at him with clear and appraising eyes.

"Where's your dad?" he asked. He turned and

saw the caretaker coming out from behind the gift shop. "There you are."

Carlo, his eyes brightening, bent to his child. "Dirty as a bug," he said.

It was nearly noon before any nuns came back, robes gray with dust, each looking more irritated and disappointed than the last. In the next half hour more nuns merged with the first flock. A few clutched tiny black change purses, filled with their measly allowances for the giftshop's medals and holy cards. In the tea room the nuns took the hard biscuits that Carlo—his daughter now nowhere in sight—set on the trestle tables. One of the oldest nuns mumbled a prayer whereupon the others bent to their biscuits. Soon they turned their faces to Jake expectantly. He had a function: to take them back to the mainland. Suddenly he was in their good graces.

When the boat was loaded and the nuns settled in and managed their robes, tossing back swathes of dark cloth, he was looking for his nun. The women kept lifting their feet from the thin scrim of saltwater on the floor of the boat.

"The other one—there was one more of you," Jake told them.

The nuns counted themselves and twice came up with the wrong number. The count was right, they said at last. Not one of their number, they insisted, was missing. Eleven of us.

He headed back up the trail, expecting to see

his little nun traipsing down, holding her gown to avoid tripping. He looked forward to watching her face change tints in embarrassment for keeping them waiting. In case she'd taken a lower path he turned back at the first twist between shrubs, shaded his eyes, and peered down at the boat rocking in a swell at the dock. Kip was standing on the third bench and staring up at him. The nuns were clustered, their hands waving. It looked like they were counting themselves again.

Just below the trail to the summit Jake passed into the chapel and breathed in its smell of smoking wax. A shadow peeled from the wall—his own. He popped into the gift shop and asked Carlo if he'd seen one more nun. The caretaker only shook his head as he picked up a creamer to stow away in the mini refrigerator. From behind the counter his little girl peered at Jake.

The wind behind the chapel was as strong as a human hand pushing at the small of his back. Ahead of him the light burned so brightly that his eyes stung. Everywhere he looked—at the dark ground, at boulders, at the stunted pines—turned black even after he blinked.

Then he saw her. Her back was to him. She stood perilously close to the edge of an outcropping. Her veil billowed behind her, folds lifting until the fabric shot back like a cartoon drawing of a speeder. He checked himself before calling out. She was near the cliff's edge. He knew better than to startle her. The sun dazzled the rocks and created a ripple in his vision. He drew the heels of his hands to his eyes.

After he pulled his hands away he blinked, his eyes burning, and the world sliding off—a thickness like egg white. He saw the nun's black form momentarily and then nothing at the spot where she had been standing.

He ran, reached the cliff, and threw himself on the ground to peer over the edge—in case the ground had collapsed. He expected, with horror, to see her gown flying in the wind. In his mind she would still be fluttering downward. He could not allow himself to imagine her body broken on the rocks below or sucked into the tide.

No wrinkling bat wing of her habit; no body. He scanned the beach. He looked out to the tide marks and further out to see if a wave had already dragged her away.

Everything was as before: the water seething with a foamy tide and then going clear near the shore, darker farther out, the air above the water finely grained, the light dazzling. He stood and walked backward and spun. Could she have taken off, run from him? Or was her body lodged between rocks on the cliffside, straight down and invisible from this height?

Jake sped to the beach and scoured every crevice before returning to the boat. He dreaded telling the nuns. For the next minute they caught his hysterics, counting and recounting their number, but before the second count he was running off again, satisfied for himself that she hadn't somehow re-emerged among them. Kip was following his orders to radio the Coast Guard. Again Jake ran to see if he had missed the nun's body between the rocks or entangled on an outcropping, saved by her outrageous robes, caught on a ragged promontory on the way down.

He took another path to the top of the cliff behind the chapel. Sea hawks skirled below him. The shadows of clouds folded in the water, and a seaweed island wavered and dipped. He stumble-ran his way to the shore, took off his boots, and dove. The water was clear and the sand on the bottom looked golden. He treaded water and peered up, shading his eyes, studying the cliff which loomed above him, velvety black. He scanned the cliff again before straggling up to a higher cliff to see if he could spot her body farther out from shore.

The nuns had determined, firmly, that they were all accounted for. Jake made a mistake if he believed any nun fitting his description arrived with them. They were a private party—no one came but themselves. Jake asked, Didn't you see when I stepped on her costume? His voice sounded pleading and strange to him, and he noticed how they bristled at *costume*. Kip didn't catch his eye, not even Kip, who was never anything but loyal.

When the thump of the Coast Guard helicopter could be heard coming from Lewinsburg he imagined that the nun would be found. On the shore again he watched the waves and saw her—her strange face and an arm rising from the ocean. An illusion, his eyes playing tricks.

Later, when he was quizzed and filled out a report on the Coast Guard cutter, he realized that both officers doubted him and that the nuns, who were closely questioned, were embarrassed, caught between pity for him and growing outrage.

Jake was thinking that some secret despair was at the root of everything. His little nun had been odd from the start, the way she hung back. He hadn't seen her talking to the others, but then, by and large, they weren't a talkative bunch. Their awareness was inward, even cold, reinforced by their medieval attachment to a weird style of dress.

A nun with a worry line that looked drawn on her forehead began talking to him about her cornea operation. Gradually he realized she was suggesting he needed to get his eyes checked. As if considerable Coast Guard expense had been devoted to an optical illusion involving sunspots. Wasn't he confused? And couldn't he have seen a shadow? Was his health all right? He suspected, too, that the nuns thought he believed that they all looked too much alike—which wasn't quite true anymore. He forced himself to look again from face to face, gargoyle to gargoyle, it seemed to him then, to try to find her as they insisted once again that they were entirely accounted for, every single one. The Coast Guard helicopter buzzed lower. Kip went off scouring the shore but kept shaking his head as he trudged back to the boat. He couldn't help himself. Kip didn't remember the nun either, and all of Jake's descriptions caused him to wrinkle up his forehead or widen his eyes in a way that made Jake think of a concerned collie.

The sea was calm as pudding, thick looking, hardly puckering by the time Jake and Kip took the nuns back to Truror. A few of the nuns surreptitiously cast glances—curious, no longer annoyed, but excited by the adventure to the point of letting their shoes get sloshed by seawater.

That night in his skiff Jake steered around the island, in and out of coves. After docking he walked the shore with a flashlight. He sat for a while on the black gravel beach, waiting for the tide to bring the woman's body in. He kept seeing her. Then kept shaking himself into consciousness.

The most likely explanation: She was there, among the other nuns when he came back to the boat. She had become one of them, drawn in by some power—gone into camouflage so that he couldn't recognize her. A magic act in reverse. She'd become ordinary, indistinguishable—and what he had seen on the cliffside was not her, was no one, but a hallucination born out of his loneliness. A woman disappearing. No, he trusted his own eyes and his own instincts. She was with them on the ride over. She had disappeared from sight at the cliff's edge. She had not returned with them. No one missed her or remembered her. But he did.

3

On Monday there were no tourists to take to the island. If his nun wasn't an apparition—and Jake didn't believe in apparitions—and she hadn't somehow squeaked away, she might still be planted there, on the island. Either her body or her living person. He walked the beaches, expecting to find her in a tangle of sea wrack or in a deeply submerged rock riddled with hollows. He swam out and the current tugged until he had to struggle his way to shore, scraping both his hands and banging up his knee as he crawled out.

He returned to the cliff where he'd seen the nun disappear and retraced his steps, recreating his body's movements the way he remembered them. Plowing up quickly with excitement at the sight of her. And then, as the sunlight slammed in his face, he had pulled up short. Could the problem be there, precisely in that instant? A gnarled shrub roughly at a human height was little more than seven yards ahead of him. In his desire to find the nun, could his eyes have created an illusion? Even now his line of sight shifted as if a wave bent through the air. What the one old nun had said about her eyes. A cornea displacement—was there such a thing? Could that account for it? He screwed up his face and rubbed his eyes and opened them again quickly. Nothing jumped.

If the nun hadn't dropped from the cliff, what could explain the fact that she wasn't on the boat? He'd gone from face to face, each stubborn in its singularity. When one of the smallest nuns turned he thought he'd found her—until he saw the woman's distinct blonde eyelashes, grey-blue eyes, almost lipless mouth. Not her. Not at all.

Jake took the skiff back to Truror, peeled off his shirt, and walked into the water in the cove on the west side of Purefoy Beach to float on his back and let his anxiety boil down. He had to have been mistaken—it was easiest to believe he had made an error. On the shore he pulled his shirt back over his head and fought against the fabric where it clung to his wet shoulders.

The carved Triton prowhead held up the television. The antique gas lanterns hung wadded in nets. The big rusted mermaid was settling sideways, ready to slide off the wall and prostrate herself on the floor boards.

Duke Githers threw himself onto a chair, planted his elbows on the table, and made a moony face. "I've been hearing rumors about you."

"Oh yeah?" Jake said, knowing he was in for it. The flying nun. And then there were nun, because there weren't any to begin with. He couldn't expect less.

The walls of Drury's Pub made him think of a singed lung. Generations of smokers. Who knew the walls' original shade? The bar was steeped in every time period of its long life. It was fine about an Applebee's coming across town as long as the bar remained the same, like some time machine the men he knew could step into and be immediately transported back into their fathers' era.

"Heard you saw something."

Jake took a good swallow of his beer. The bitterness struck his palate and helped him ignore Duke.

There was a residue of pity in Duke's voice. Vague suspicion, too. Jake had never stayed anywhere for long—had tried to be quiet, unobtrusive, an invisible boy in each foster home. Early on he'd cycled through families in Truror until he was sent outside town, twice to homes farther inland than seventy miles. His mother's friend, Mrs. Cu, managed the house left to him and allowed for occasional renters, but with taxes and her fee and the expenses of upkeep, Jake had little more than the property itself to call his own when, after high school, he returned to Truror. Some of his mother's things were left for him, out of storage and unpacked, apparently, by Mrs. Cu. The bedspread was returned to the room that had been his mother's. He had wanted to be grateful for that.

For two years he stayed, long enough to save money from working on the boats to leave again and try to get a useless degree in classics that in the end he couldn't afford. At Luxenburg he met the woman who would become his wife, then worked at three credit unions before the divorce and his return to Truror. Still, returning wasn't enough for people like Duke. Jake could not make up for the years he chose to live elsewhere after he returned the first time—and even for the years after his mother's death when he was shuttled between far-flung families, when never asking for seconds at the dinner table and never getting less than decent grades could not forestall the next arrangement, another home where he was a stranger.

"Don't worry," Duke said. "People see things. You know you're the real thing if you start having visions. You should be a priest for that. Or a monk. God help us if you're a monk."

"Next it's a mermaid," Jake said, as if joining in the joke. He felt sick for betraying himself. Owen Pasteur ambled over and sat down beside him.

Duke must have guessed Jake's misery. "If you saw what you think you did, my bet is that they'll find her yet... her body, anyway. But a nun—you have to realize those nuns keep track of each other. They may look no more different from one another—to us—than eggs, but they recognize one another. Although it might be that you're right and she snuck on your boat. Maybe from another order."

"She snuck on...because she had a mission,"

Owen said. "To scare the hell out of you. Or it was a conspiracy. A conspiracy on the part of those nuns. They were leaving her behind, growing their own convent's saint."

Kip was at the pool table with a girl, her sunburned belly rising out of her too-tight jeans in a little luminous spare tire. When she bent with her pool stick, her hair fell forward, blonde with black roots. It seemed like she planned it that way, the effect too stark to be otherwise.

Jake remembered her name: Brittany. The girl could no more play pool than Kip could conduct an orchestra. Leaning over the table for another shot, her shyness was practically turning into steam. Did Kip know she was crazy about him?

The girl straightened up, adjusting her blouse, her belly springing again like a breathing comical thing. Later Kip had one arm draped over her shoulder. She was swaying against him, the pool cue propped against the table.

Duke wasn't done. "She's still there; that could be. You said there was something in your eye— somebody said that anyway—and in that amount of time…she's little, someone said you said—a little sister, short—she got herself behind you and sped off like the wind."

Jake knew he wouldn't believe himself, either.

"Then," Owen interjected, "she got on her dirt bike and jumped the cliff and sped off on her glider never to be seen again. Until she was discovered working the docks with her pimp Lars."

"It's good you're back," Duke said. "You can count on full sympathy from some of us."

"Who hasn't seen something on the water?" Owen said, sounding almost contrite.

"There were stories about why you left…."

As if it wasn't enough to live close to the ocean, as if it wasn't natural to duplicate their ritual nights at a bar with the television posted near the ceiling, alongside the pasteboard mermaid and old tackle. With these guys you were disloyal if you weren't conspiratorial about the prospect of another hardware opening or muttering that Luther Eartll's diabetes gave him an unfair advantage. But you didn't talk about going home to a wife bored beyond her years and irritable from the children's needs and drawing back at the smell in your hair—something she could not choose to grow accustomed to. The sun felt like it was still sunk around your eyes where the skin withered. You were owned by your beers, and paid some minimal bar tax. And you thought you knew the saga of Jake's ex-wife—who had visited Truror to look at the property left in trust to him by his mother and went so far as to show off her disappointment.

Another possibility came to Duke: "Maybe—just maybe—they weren't nuns. Not a single one of them."

"Like maybe they were bank robbers disguised as nuns. Freak."

"But didn't it strike you as strange that they were in full habits? Kip said they were dressed, all of them, in full habits. Who does that anymore? And aren't there usually at least a few in a group who rebel? Aren't they usually dressed in half veils, with skirts, what do you call that kind of skirt ... A-line skirts. Don't laugh at me. I have sisters."

Kip jogged up to the table. "We've seen our share of nuns," he said. The girl wasn't with him. "We kind of recognize the uniform."

"All right then. But special nuns. Strange nuns. Nuns attached to the past. Dated nuns."

"Who dates a nun?" Owen joked.

Another round of beers came out.

"Mine's alive," Kip said, meaning his beer. He set the glass down, splattering foam. The girl was watching him from the other side of the pool table.

Jake wondered if Kip knew what he was getting into. He had never seen a young woman like that—as set on Kip. He was a good looking kid and had that laughter in his nature, rare because it wasn't mean-spirited. You'd think a kid like that would observe what he was doing to that girl. Kip trotted back and poked her in the belly.

"Who is she?"

At first Jake thought Duke was asking about Brittany, the bare-bellied girl. But then he looked around to see who Duke was talking about. His eyes snagged on a girl whose skin was a color that struck him as made in a tanning bed. A straight nose, a narrow, fox-like face. He followed the light of her eyes to Kip, who was leaning again over Brittany at the pool table. Brittany, with the pool stick, was pretending to shove him.

Jake didn't think much of it until later when Brittany left for work at Hoy's and the new girl with the thin face sidled up to Kip. He could hope that Kip would brush her off. Watching felt a little perverted, though at least he wasn't the only pervert. The attention of the other men in the bar was tightening, too, even if they were careful to keep their heads screwed straight on. The volume in the bar had come down in response to the girl's cool laughter. She bore an uncanny resemblance to Jake's former wife. That couldn't be her fault. About Brittany—he supposed those belly-baring shirts of hers made her look even younger than she was, that little satiny pad of flesh simultaneously endearing and pathetic. Whereas this new girl. He worried about Kip, not about her. And maybe envied Kip, too.

4

A slight Japanese woman brought out a small paisley purse and rummaged in it as the boat rose and dipped precipitously. She extracted plastic baggies which she offered to other passengers before delicately vomiting into her own. Soon enough there was a break in the stacked clouds and the island was shoveled toward them, the summit obscured by another cloud mass.

They were mostly an international group this time: three Poles, two Russians, four Japanese. There was just one American couple and their little boy, all three looking bored. Jake sensed the others on the boat feigning either understanding or interest as he detailed the history and pervasive uncertainty attached to the island.

"The Flying Island got its name, as far as we can tell, because of an optical illusion that's not quite visible today. In certain sorts of weather the island does look like it's floating. The crown of the island floats—."

"Why isn't it called the floating island?" It was the American couple's son. Red hair like a dye job. The boy had to be no older than ten.

"That would work," Jake said.

"Then why not?"

"Because the island under certain conditions looks like it's coming right at you." He was tempted to clap his hands in the boy's face.

"No it doesn't."

"Only for some people," Jake said. "The smart ones."

The kid's dad didn't look happy. Why add to the sum total of human misery?

"Like you."

The boy laughed in Jake's face, and his parents joined in. Knowing laughter.

Jake wondered, before quickly turning away from the thought, if he wasn't a figure of fun to too many people and if he shouldn't take the matter seriously. If he became that way to himself, if he settled into that role, even to himself—wouldn't he have wasted his life, wasted whatever was good in him? Whatever authority he had to call his life genuine? Let them laugh. He didn't know what they wanted him to know.

A white-haired woman on the second bench of the boat held her head back, her eyes closed, preferring a more private vista than the curdling water. When they pulled into shore she was humming loudly enough to be annoying. By then Jake realized she was blind. She was led by a friend to the summit—and would not accept his or Kip's help—and afterwards Jake waited to see if her face would change. What could she experience other than patches of warming sunlight, the wind like a long whip? Later he stood to watch her coming down step by step, at an angle, one foot dabbing at each step, as if feeling for wet paint.

At last, when her companion—a man older than she and with giant liver patches on each cheek—led her gropingly to the table for tea and biscuits Jake was rewarded: her trembling hands, everything tremulous, the little muscles of her face more alive than anything he had seen since his nun.

It would have to be a window banging, the sound loud enough that it seemed engineered by anger. The shadow passed over his head. He went into what had been his mother's room and caught the window as it was about to crack against the frame. He could hear the bird's wings rubbing together like dry papers. Its shadow was like a Japanese fan cast on the wall. The bird landed on a coat tree. The oval mirror reflected the window and the tree outside. He stationed himself in front of the glass and waved his arms to keep the bird from mistaking the mirror for the world.

The bird flew in a bobbing path as if riding an invisible wave toward the upper glass pane before, at the last instant, diving into free air.

The island was visible from the window—a soft

black dot, a raised mole.

He'd at least kept the house that had been held as his legacy. Virtually everything else went to his ex-wife. He was glad, as if it amounted to penance. He'd fooled her after all, trying to be more outgoing and challenging, playacting intense interest in things that filled him with dread and boredom—séances, tours of historical homes, concerts of sadsack singers who leavened their lyrics with ironies he hadn't enjoyed since he was fourteen.

His marriage amounted to a blank, writhing shame. He had floated after her, convinced by the apparent passion of her own responses and by her good little body. He had wanted to make her happy, that much was certain. The more he tried, the less happy she was, and the more he felt like an uninvited guest at the dining room table until he found himself eating alone anyway. Afterwards he threw over what remained of his life and returned to Truror.

He shut the window. When he turned back he saw his mother's bedspread had turned a pale green, bleached by years of window light.

That night the fox-faced girl was at the bar again. She was staying at the vacation home her parents rented, Jake learned. She was with a friend, which made her plans all the more obvious. A strategy for the two of them—the heavier one jostling against the skinny intense girl and Kip oblivious at first even when the fox-faced girl sauntered over, touched his elbow. She was a beautiful girl, probably more beautiful at close range. Jake felt he was watching something ancient—the blood rising in Kip's face, his mannerisms writhing with self-consciousness, the girl taking his hand and leading him out of the bar in front of everyone, Kip's face darkening even more under his thatch of black hair and the girl with her long thin triumphant arm extended, unshadowed, like a brown lithe creature that almost seemed apart from her. It was like watching a succubus about to get to work. How could Kip defend himself?

In the morning Jake slept so late that Kip, still apparently buzzed, rang the bell to get him up. By then, Jake was ready to take another boatful out—laypeople, mostly amiable-seeming senior citizens—and he made sure that Kip began with the spiel about the island, knowing that this lot of passengers probably wouldn't mind the level of uncertainty that a true account of the island required.

His face strained in a hard wind for hours, and that night he was repaid with drowsiness. Before he got into bed he hadn't even noticed how wet he was, not until he unbuttoned his shirt and began peeling it off, a clinging second skin that he wrung out over the tub. He slept poorly and kept waking, blaming the moon and the wet boat ride back to the mainland. He had been soaked to the skin and careless. The island was buried in clouds—unable to fly, vanished.

5

Jake caught a full view when Mrs. Cu came out of the pharmacy swinging two plastic bags and walking in the way he'd remembered as a boy—wide-legged. Her way of moving could, he supposed, appear childlike, but it made him think of bullying.

She had been his mother's friend, no matter the number of times his mother expressed irritation at her. He could even remember a time—early on—when his mother avoided her calls. Throughout his mother's life, or the slice of it Jake knew about, Mrs. Cu came to visit, and after the trauma of his father's abandonment Mrs. Cu, clutching her sewing basket and her enormous plaid purse, entered the house all the more, with her smell of yeast and lilies of the valley. Despite the fact that in his dreams over the years she had assumed the form of all sorts of creatures, including a fly hovering over a cat's corpse, he believed that in a fair assessment she had been only bent on kindness, meddling and muddling her way into and through his mother's days.

A bad hip, he thought, that's what accounted for the greater than ever exaggeration in her gait. If she wasn't nearly at her car he would have bounded across the street to help her with her bags.

The dark ovals of her sunglasses flashed. Then she was in the driver's seat and backing out of her parking space in the opposite direction, away from him. He felt a tug at his shoulder, a hand clasping and tightening. "She's too old for you, buddy." It was Duke, who seemed—bizarrely enough—serious.

Mrs. Gustuf was leaning her head back to watch a retrospective on NASCAR. He might as well be a ghost for the amount of attention she gave him. At last she drew back and pulled a Corona out of the refrigerator compartment. Devereaux Le Mann was the only other customer at Drury's, and he had to be close to ninety.

The door banged. It was the caretaker, Carlo, who must have caught a ride with Doug Llewellyn's boat into Truror. Jake wondered who was watching the little girl. He knew the rumors about Carlo. That he was a weird duck. That his salary was arranged through the office of the Truror Pump House. That his wife had died. There were rumors that she dropped to her death from one of the island's cliffs. You have to tolerate a little shoving in a marriage, people said, and with a cliff outside the door, what was to be expected? But no: ovarian cancer.

Carlo got Mrs. Gustuf's attention, then carried

over his glass with his hand cupped at the top, like the beer was a vigil light, like a breeze might blow off the foam. He sat at the next table and craned his neck toward the television before he said, "Any more ideas about what you saw?"

Mrs. Gustuf trundled over and bent to Jake before he could answer. "You know what I like about you?" she asked. "You never look like you're angry because I'm a disappointment."

"You couldn't disappoint me."

"That's very nice to hear, let me tell you. Carlo, you're like that, too. I never feel like I have to wear high boots to get your friendship."

When Mrs. Gustuf plodded back to the bar, Carlo asked Jake, "No one's giving you a hard time about what you saw, are they?"

Before Jake could answer, Carlo kept on: "There could be a good explanation. I mean—an explanation that would make sense. We can't know what these things mean. Or maybe it's nothing. The air and the light up there play tricks."

He was speaking so rapidly with strange intakes of breath—like choking gulps—that Jake felt sure the caretaker was holding something back.

"What tricks have they played on you?" he asked.

Carlo didn't answer and instead said, "Why do you think you saw what you did?" Jake had come up with some possibilities, each more unsettling than the last.

One: that the nuns purposefully came out to the island because his nun would take her life on the cliffs. She was disgraced—perhaps with a pregnancy?—and blamed by the other nuns and thus shamed into ending her life. Another scenario: a suicide from simple despair, her body swept out to sea immediately. Although that seemed too quick for him to have seen nothing at all.

More often, he kept imagining his nun's body caught between rocks as she plummeted down the cliff, her long gown tangled in a crevice and twisted until she was swaddled tight as a fly in a spider web. Shadows might make her body invisible from the cliff or even from the shore.

Or, he had seen someone else. There was someone else on the island who had arrived with the nuns, blending in. She was still there—and in the seconds when his vision wavered and rippled, and he saw like a ribbon in a marble the nun's veil, his eyes stinging, when a corona of flares broke his vision, and then he saw nothing where she had stood....

Jake had no answers, no way to explain himself, but found himself asking, "Your daughter? Could it be her?"

"You're an idiot," Carlo said, slamming his chair back. In an instant his face softened. "Sorry," he said.

"I should be sorry," Jake said. "A stupid thing to say. Sorry."

He liked that the caretaker wasn't from the island or even from Truror or Quinnippeg but from Toronto, had met his wife there. She was from Truror, a daughter, in fact, of Bertrand Squires—an institution more than a man, and deeply appreciated as one of the few decent lawyers locally. In fact people still invoked him in cases where integrity was referred to: the late Bertrand Squires. Jake thought he remembered Carlo's wife from the lower grades. The strangeness he saw in her little daughter's face might not be so strange after all. It could be the juncture of one memory meeting another half-forgotten one.

He considered telling Carlo about the sect that buried baby clothes and felt some constraint. Carlo didn't need to be reminded of women or death.

6

It looked like a sloppy bundle tumbling down the hillside and then Jake realized: It was one of his passengers. The shortest man on the boat was falling down the steps from the island's summit. By the time Jake reached the man a shrub had halted his fall. The poor guy popped up, his face scratched with thin lines as if he'd slept overnight with a leaky red pen. He looked otherwise uninjured except in the region of the elbows.

"It's nothing," the man said, wincing while Kip jogged over, sucking his teeth.

Jake scrambled up the steps and found one of the stones dislodged. Kip waited by the crumbling step while Jake clambered up to warn the remaining group—a family extended predominantly by uncles. The steps would have to be re-cemented. He and Kip took hold of the arms of their passengers as they worked their way past the bad step. When the last tourists were down, Jake sprinted to the cottage and looked for Carlo to warn him but didn't find him. He was staring at the steps when he saw the caretaker's little girl making her way toward the summit.

The wind picked up his voice and sent it back to him as he called to her. The child might lose her footing even without the loose step. He could have shot himself for not putting up a warning marker, a flag, as if they had a flag. Or a shirt even. He was angry at Carlo for letting the girl run free. Like a feral cat. You could practically roll out of bed and wind up in the ocean at a place like this. As he ran after the child he called to her again. She was a white shadow moving in a straight vertical path.

She stopped and turned. The broken step was two above her. He tried to keep his face calm, not to frighten her, but he feared he hadn't succeeded. She turned and this time thrust herself into the air. He leaned, stumbling, catching her low, her neck and head almost grazing the rocks. Her body folded between his arms. In his horror and fury—was she trying to *die*?—he shouted, a shout that was unintelligible, followed by a huffing groan like a bear's. Then he was deaf to anything but the blood pounding in his ears.

He waited at the trestle table, his shirt soaked with sweat. When the little girl came back out from the cottage she was carrying tiny tea things on a platter—as if he were one of her dolls. Neither he nor the child spoke. He pretended to drink from the empty cup she gave him, his hands shaking badly.

7

Wooden frames leaned against the wall in a room off the main living space of Carlo's cottage. Canvases. It seemed likely that the caretaker was a secret artist. That would account for his willingness to take on such a desolate job, just for the air and the quality of light.

"You're all right?" Carlo asked.

Jake wished he hadn't accepted his invitation. But Carlo had pressed it on him, grateful that he'd saved his little girl. Ginny.

The kettle began a soft burble. The caretaker got up, talking fast as if to cover his own embarrassment for not watching more closely after his daughter. "I heard from someone that to make a good pot of tea you have to catch the kettle right before it boils. It has to do with the oxygen." When Carlo came back to the living area he paused before plunging ahead. "Tell me again what she looked like?" he asked. "Maybe I saw her after all—with the rest of them." Carlo was talking about the nun.

What could Jake say that didn't sound ridiculous? Eyes like metal. Practically swimming in her clothes. The rest of the nuns kept away from her— she had that effect on them. What else could he say?

Some element of what Jake had seen on the cliff when the nun dropped—if she had dropped— thrashed in his mind. Her back had elongated slightly, just for a split second. Taking a breath; that was what she was doing just before she disappeared. Swallowing as much air as she could.

Something else occurred to Jake as Carlo settled back into his chair with his own cup.

"You've seen weird things, too?" Jake asked.

Carlo set his cup down. He took a while to answer. "Oh yeah," he said.

"Yeah?"

"Oh yeah."

Jake sat waiting, feeling his irritation mount. Nice not to be the only lunatic. But now Carlo was turning the conversation away and back to his child. "We thought I'd be off the island before she needed school."

"How old is she?"

"Nine. Home schooling is crap. When I'm doing it, anyway. She has to go to school in the fall. No more home schooling."

"Truror is all right for school. A lot of us survived it at her age."

"If I don't get another job she'll be staying with Lorraine. Her aunt. Lorraine has her own life though. It's a lot to ask of her. And honestly I don't know—."

It was none of his business, Jake was thinking. If he a had a child and someone told him how to raise it he wouldn't be charitable—except that Carlo seemed eager to talk. Maybe not having a wife anymore made him that way. Who else could he talk to about Ginny?

Carlo said, "There's not much for her on the island."

"Where is she now?"

"With Lorraine. Sometimes I think she'd be better off with her all the time."

Carlo said he caught Ginny on the steps to the summit only a week before, pumping her arms in the air as if she could fly, and so when Jake told him about the incident on the steps—how she threw herself into his arms and nearly killed them both—Carlo sent her off to Lorraine's again. To give himself time to think. To keep her safe.

"You could leave the island."

"I've been trying. I have my résumé out."

Jake wondered what kind of résumé Carlo could have. What job would he possibly be suited for? Lighthouse keeper? Hermit? Carlo was looking guilty and sheepish.

"I try," he said.

Jake imagined it was very different when Carlo's wife was alive.

"Mine was a monk."

"What?" Jake asked.

"He was there and then he wasn't. He even had a tonsure. Not a natural bald spot. A tonsure. Except I didn't call the Coast Guard. I just doubted myself. It didn't seem real even while it was happening."

A monk had evaporated into air. A year ago.

"I didn't send out a search party. You went further."

"Your monk probably wasn't on a cliff."

"Damn near."

"So," Jake said after a while. "How do you explain it?"

"Until your episode I just counted it as a problem of my own—a hallucination."

8

The beach sand was packed hard from rain. Pipers made screeches: *what have I lost? what have I lost?*

He had no idea what to make of it, how it was that the caretaker had seen something equally bizarre...and he had even less of an idea why Carlo had trusted him with it. He still couldn't get over how readily Carlo had taken him into his confidence. His apparition had secured him a friend. Unidentified flying religious orders. But the monk Carlo had seen.... Jake let his mind play with the absurdity. As if the island were like an elephant graveyard for religious people—they came here to die or to leave tusks in the form of spooky visions. He should have asked Carlo more: How old was the monk? Who brought him over? Doug Llewellyn and that crew?

The Flying Island. He'd read his Jonathan Swift. That island was not like this island.

People don't fly off cliffs. They fall off cliffs.

The sea was rain-pocked, the entire expanse of water dimpled. As Jake watched, the water began turning into jade and marble, something that belonged in an old woman's china cabinet. To the west the horizon faded. Light broke through, the clouds slowly growing visible out of a pearly grey.

In the surf a man wagged his head to get water out of his ears. A young woman—his daughter?—jumped the waves and popped up like a cork. Fewer than twenty yards from Jake a cluster of teenage girls raised their voices, kicking about in the sand, intent on drawing attention to their innocently wild selves.

In the afternoon Jake took the skiff to the island to search for the nun's body again, knowing he was working from instinct and not logic. If the nun had fallen from the cliff her body could be far out to sea or as likely to wash up at Truror as anywhere on the island.

The light dimmed under limestone where a natural stone bridge arched only inches above Jake's head. Below, past where the path ended, waves caromed into a hollow and, after a pause, cannoned out again, as if some dramatic transformation took place in that split moment of silence. As his eyes grew accustomed to the shadows he imagined finding his nun's body—torn and hideous, a veil washing in and out, inflating like a bladder. He hoped that Carlo had warned Ginny against this place.

The sea had carved out a cave even further below in the limestone. The pit was like a chambered nautilus. Leaning forward he kept his balance only precariously by clawing at a rock face. Under the boom of the sea he heard voices echoing, a woman's high and demanding, then wheedling.

Lower, a man's quieter voice, distorted. It was Kip.

Jake edged back and made his way up. Someone—Wordsworth or someone—had once said that no man can be unhappy looking into the distance. When he got to solid ground he looked toward the horizon. Wordsworth, or whoever it was, was a fool.

9

It was still late afternoon and the sun held an almost
mentholated chill, as if the wind came from some
far-off region, filtered through ferns and scrubbed
on sun-blasted rocks. He was searching tide line
caves. As a kid—he couldn't have been older than
nine—Jake spent the night in the highest cave and
woke up to find his face wet and the ocean only
yards below him. Through the barrel blasts of the
incoming tide, he hadn't even woken for a moment. The cave became a monstrous maw for him,
darkly inviting. No one knew where he was. He
was beyond any of them, even his mother's friend,
Mrs. Cu, who had set herself up as a nearly perma-
nent sentinel in his home. All those years ago he
had curled up on the cave floor and pulled himself
out the next morning, hanging from the outer lip
and dropping to a sandstone ledge before fumbling
back to a solid path that led to the higher elevation
behind the chapel.

Jake stepped over loose stones and found a path

that would eventually curve around to the cave. A stone flew from under his boot with as much force as if he'd punted it. It seemed unlikely anyone would have attempted to enter the cave in recent years. Erosion had narrowed the ledge.

Focusing inches beyond his feet, he tried to keep his balance. He could turn back before the path got any trickier—if his curiosity weren't luring him.

For the past week and a half he had scoured much of the island, rediscovering it in the process. Its rock faces wrinkled as walnuts or slick as black glass. Its mossy outcroppings. The foamy inlet near the last string of abandoned cottages. Repeatedly, he felt he was coming upon some mystery that defied him, disappearing when he approached, breaking up like a million winged insects.

Only a yard from the mouth of the cave the trail crumbled. Rocks and soil had fallen from the ledge. The cave looked almost impassable. He told himself he should have taken the skiff around, spied the cave with binoculars, although given the angle it was unlikely he would have been able to discover much.

Under his right boot the earth gave. He braced against the wall and concentrated on the sensation of heat on his back muscles to keep from losing his equilibrium. He took his chance then, stretching his right leg past the break in the path. He clung to the rock face and drew his left leg away. He rolled forward and into the cave, his shoulder cracking against stone. He sat up, hugged his shoulder, huffing off breaths of pain before he filled with elation.

How he would get out and down he didn't know. He was just glad his skull was intact. Inches from his feet was pure air—and ocean light dimming steadily, a lid clamping on the horizon. He was surprised to see blood on his pants. He realized that his legs had been scraped in his contortions to get into the cave.

As light disappeared the cave began to feel more like a crawl space. Hunched, he turned his back on the ocean. The worst he had to fear would be hawks or bats. Carefully, he stretched out his legs and drew back. Supposing the ocean had risen since he was a kid? He'd be washed out by morning. He felt around in the dark and was reassured—the walls were cool but dry. He breathed in the sharp memory of wanting to disappear here all those years ago. The nun's vanishing from sight might have been just that—he had felt her wish to disappear, had intuited it so sharply that he had imagined it all. Or maybe, after all, she had returned to the boat but turned off her beautiful high-wattage intensity entirely. Maybe that had been why he couldn't find her. She had returned in disguise—as one of the others, no different, no more alive.

Once dawn arrived, he would have to see if there were any routes on the other side of the cave or even above it. He would have to find a way to scramble out without dropping into the ocean.

He leaned back on his elbows. Instantly he jerked forward, all his instincts buzzing.

Under his elbow: a wad of hair—soft hair.

He could feel the hair stickily brushing against his skin, silkier, not like an animal's. When he could control his revulsion he made himself pat his hands around in the darkness. He pulled the hair and with it came something dangling.

A doll, thin, knifelike. A naked little doll.

10

"Is this yours?"

Jake knelt and handed the doll to Ginny. She looked into his face and then at the doll and took it, pressing it against her chest before running off. He almost wanted to apologize…to let her know that he would have to betray her.

"So how could she *get* there?" Carlo was staring off toward the chapel, unable to meet Jake's eyes.

"There's a trail. Not an easy one. I nearly broke my neck once yesterday and twice this morning. And there's a jump, too. You can get onto the lower trail and swing up." It should be impossible for a little kid, Jake was thinking. He couldn't stop feeling guilty—peaching on a nine-year-old.

The implication was clear. The child was too much for Carlo. The island was filled with dangers. She was wandering off and doing bizarre things. Carlo was wildly lucky not to have lost her already.

Jake still couldn't understand how she got into the cave.

It was almost as if she'd have to be lifted.

Nevertheless, Jake wanted to warn the caretaker: Don't give away your own child. Carlo looked as if his daughter was already lost to him. And who was Jake but the messenger of doom?

He changed the subject. "Was the monk you saw—was he in a monk outfit—one of the belted outfits?"

"He was."

"Was it too big for him?"

"I don't know. Aren't they all too big for them? Belted like that, you know?"

But Carlo seemed distracted, his mind surely on his daughter. And his failures.

11

When Jake came up the path to the cottage, the child, wearing a white dress, heavily smudged, was sitting on the stone wall. She jumped down and stood motionless, staring at him. Her face was grey with dirt. She must have been playing in her garden again. He wanted to talk to her but it seemed better to nod. Ginny nodded back and ran ahead, opening the cottage door.

The coolness inside the cottage rushed over him, as if he were walking into a root cellar. Carlo rose and clasped his hand then stepped back. At first Jake couldn't make out the form behind Carlo in the big armchair until the form pushed up from the chair—Jake caught an impression of slenderness and pale-brown hair—and came into better light. Carlo introduced them. His wife's sister, the one who often took care of Ginny. Ginny, who had been near the door, came forward and stood in front of her aunt.

"She made it," Ginny said.

"What?"

"She made my dress."

Lorraine was not known to him—not remembered—which seemed impossible, given that he vaguely remembered her sister. But then he learned from Carlo that her family had relatives in town; her mother had "married out," and Lorraine was the youngest from the second marriage after Squires's death. For the sake of her mother Lorraine never moved far from the coast, although her prospects might have been better elsewhere.

The child wriggled in close to her, clamping a hand on her aunt's skirt. The aunt smiled at Jake but the smile was shrinking. Later he considered the possibility that her expression had altered because he hadn't smiled in return but stood there, dumbfounded, heaving with stupidity.

There was a lot of rice in whatever it was that Carlo baked and some kind of fish although so heavily seasoned and minced that Jake wasn't entirely sure what he was eating. The table wasn't meant for an extra person of his size. He tucked his elbows close and focused on controlling his fork. Even so, rice grains kept sliding off his plate as if magnetized. Halfway through the meal Ginny reached over and patted his hand, patted him as if he were a dog or some other nervous but harmless animal. He felt pride. If Ginny cared for him it could be a signal to Lorraine that he wasn't worthless.

The woman seemed quiet but unusually alert—observant. Sneaking a glance at her during dinner he saw she wasn't even looking at him. He had only imagined he was being watched. He wondered if Carlo might be attracted to her. And yet the two of them seemed more like a brother and sister than in-laws—they were that easy together, with a mild note of teasing in their voices. They had talked about him, he was sure. He wondered if Carlo had told her about the incident with the nun—the one most likely to be considered imaginary.

"Ginny is an unusual girl," Lorraine said as she and Jake, after dinner, were walking past the chapel. Lorraine, he realized, reminded him of a seal—dark eyes with stiff lashes set far apart, a look of curiosity without aggression. He knew better than to mention the resemblance. Lorraine was still talking. "She's like my sister was. Truly. This island means too much to her."

"Your sister…I'm sorry."

"I worry about Ginny. She wanders away. He turns his back and she's gone. She needs friends her own age. I tried, but she's not interested in the other kids I've tried to set her up with."

"She seems—." He was reluctant to hazard an opinion. The look Lorraine gave him allowed him to plunge ahead. "She seems older than she is. Not that I know much about kids."

"She doesn't talk much. That's what makes her seem older. And the dolls. She doesn't really play with them."

"She buries them."

"I know." She shuddered, then laughed. "I don't know what she's up to. It's as if she knows something we don't."

"You made her dress for her?"

"She's growing so much, I'm surprised anything I made even a month ago fits her." This was why Ginny didn't dress in shorts and jeans like most girls her age, Jake realized; she wore the dresses her aunt made. He wondered if Lorraine was a lot like Ginny's mother had been.

Lorraine tilted her head in a way he was recognizing had something to do, possibly, with some problem with her eyesight. Her eyes fluttered away from his. He understood then that she was by nature shy. She might, given his status as a near-stranger and the isolation of the island, be trying out a new behavior on him by talking freely.

"Carlo used to be a lot more forthcoming," she said. "I suppose he realized there was a limit to what words could do."

"Are you coming back soon?"

"I'm committed to helping Ginny. And Carlo."

He wondered if she was trying to tell him something—that her interests were not only with her niece but with Carlo. She was "committed."

During dinner Carlo had said she was an information technologist for the library at Sandover.

"I've always liked libraries," Jake said, to change the subject, and feeling inane. He couldn't help but think of Lorraine diving into the wells of information in a library, pretending to be a normal person when she could probably tap into vast codes. She seemed so anxious to intervene in Ginny's life with Carlo, just when it appeared to Jake that the father and his child needed some time—time to make a new sort of alliance, without the impression of chronic absence between them.

He asked her to come to dinner at his house. He gave her the address in Truror so quickly that he had to repeat it twice.

She changed the subject back again. "Ginny's having a hard time, isn't she? Carlo doesn't tell me enough. I want to help them, but—." She stopped. It was clear that she felt she'd gone too far. It was their business. He felt her body stiffen beside him and wondered if she'd rebuked herself, ordered herself to pull away. Then he realized something had caught her attention.

It was Ginny she was looking toward. The child was up ahead, near the cliff's edge.

"We shouldn't startle her," he said, and then, "She seems all right." Even as he spoke he was realizing something: Ginny was not close to the edge. The shadows, the way the rim of the cliff curved—she wasn't as close to the cliff's edge as it appeared from where they stood. The distance looked foreshortened, a trick of shadows, the time of day.

12

When her white miserable little car that looked fated for accidents was at the curb Jake was only a block behind her. She was pulling out a satchel. He slowed his pace, experiencing the same inertia he had felt as a boy, as if whenever Mrs. Cu was in sight he was meant to detach, to slide away unseen inside a dark cavern, the air fuzzy around him, feeling his way forward, blind.

She gathered up her purse, draped the band of the satchel over her shoulder, and began her sideways lurch toward St. Agatha's. He waited some minutes for her to come out, telling himself, This is stupid, what are you waiting here for? Though when a few more minutes passed and she still hadn't emerged, he took the church steps in three bounds and almost staggered opening the doors. He wondered that she had the strength for it, although despite her crooked walk she conveyed a sense of tremendous will.

The smell of incense in the entranceway closed

his throat. The promise was here—he could not deny it, the inexplicable possibility of new life—and while he struggled against his conflicting impulses, walk through or turn to run, the power of whatever it was cut through him. He did not see how even Mrs. Cu could take it regularly, coming to the church. His mother had avoided the church, but that loneliness in her had been a force that drew Mrs. Cu, drew her thick stumpiness in, until his mother was powerless against her. His mother's passivity, her helpless eyes, these had drawn Mrs. Cu. Surely and soon enough Mrs. Cu fit into their lives, coming over to vacuum and dust as his mother sat staring into space. Mrs. Cu made things run—irregularly, perhaps, but just enough so that his mother could pass as his mother still. As a boy Jake did not talk to her other than a few dutiful thank yous. He was convinced she hated him more than he hated her, hated him for reasons he could not entirely fathom, unless it was his ingratitude, which he couldn't help. She'd dragged his mother away, put her in an invisible sack and dragged her away.

Of course Mrs. Cu thought herself virtuous, self-sacrificing, moral, a warrior on behalf of this broken little duo. Mrs. Cu. Purveyor of pine scented cleaning products, scrubber of messes.

Echoes from the sacristy. The sound of glass on metal. He tried to quiet his breathing, aware that every sound was amplified. As he edged toward the pillars he saw her. Polishing the candle holders beneath St. Joseph—the ignored saint, Mary's long-suffering spouse. Mrs. Cu, a shadow alive to her task. Her face was a mask of concentration, all her force gathered as if to polish the gates of paradise. A memory came back: Mrs. Cu washing his mother's face with a cloth while his mother sat upright doing nothing, staring at nothing. Did she love his mother? The thought floated away instantly, although it would resurface later. He turned, leaving as quietly as he could manage. If by stalking an old woman he had expected to find something, some hidden truth, he was disappointed.

On the sidewalk he saw what earlier he had been too focused on Mrs. Cu to notice. Her husband was in the passenger seat of the car, the escort. Bizarre to think that such a woman ever needed protection. Jake recognized the jaw on the man, larded over from the years. A bullish silent man. He felt a twinge of empathy for Mrs. Cu. It was probably loneliness that drove her to Jake's mother, Mrs. Cu sitting with her ugly pink sewing box, looking at his mother as if she were the television and ought to be more entertaining.

Later that day Jake felt a chill in his stomach, like drinking a cold beer too fast during a wind storm. The group of middle-aged hikers he and Kip took to the island were not humbled by the view from the summit, not a too-alive face among them. They weren't coming down halfway on their knees but took the steps in thick brown sandals or dirty mustard-colored hiking boots. Too vigorous by far.

There was a band that night at the Truror Oyster House—something vaguely Jamaican. The music drifted on the night air. As he walked near the pier he stopped to listen to the faint knocking of boats and the low wash of waves. The island was almost invisible, except for a far darkening across the water.

The light sputtered in the front hallway of his home and cast the living room into shadows. He was forgetting his mother, could not summon her face. He was summoning the three photographs of her that he owned, not her. Which filled him with a threat of meaninglessness so vast that the only relief, if it could be called relief, was bringing to mind the sight of her propped in the chair, no longer alive—that vision branded in his mind, unchangeable. It seemed to him that her secret was that his life as her son wasn't meaningful to her. The chair he last saw her in was pushed against the living room's back wall, its open peonies like blood stains. The first time his ex-wife came to Truror she had sat on it—as if her mere physical presence could change everything. The thought that occurred to him at the time: She thinks her own ass is the cure. Maybe with her next husband she would be right.

It was his own fault, Jake knew. During their marriage he had turned to ice. She had as much chance with him as a cough had melting a glacier. She told him it wasn't his fault, their divorce. It had to do, she said, with their breathing rhythms. He had known she'd leave him once it came down to the lungs.

She had been right about the house—it wasn't "healthy." God, she loved health. Things were healthy or unhealthy, toxic or clean. What could purge the place?

The street outside the kitchen window was empty for long stretches. When a car drove past it was only his neighbor, the one who lived three doors down, a widower, sunk in perpetual grief. He'd been like that for as long as Jake could remember. Undead, unchanging.

13

Jake washed and dried each dish and all silverware—although he'd submerged the already-clean dishes and silverware in water overnight. The house had never before seemed so mausoleum-like. It was partly a factor of the blinds in the living room—the way the light came through dun and gold, a mortuary quality that he hadn't let himself notice before. With the blinds up, the dust in the room turned to vellum. He took a roll of paper towels which, in good order, after being rubbed around an end table, looked furred.

Lorraine would arrive in a little less than an hour. The more he tidied up the more dirt showed itself. He'd deliberately left chopping peppers, onions, zucchini until the last minute. He thought they would turn to pasty mush otherwise. He looked down at his t-shirt, the same one he slept in—yellow with a slogan so faded and broken up he'd forgotten until now that it said Open 24 Hours. He pulled it off and took the quickest shower of his life, then rushed into the kitchen and set the vegetables in olive oil on low heat on the stove—and washed off and patted dry a length of cod and took another shower—when he heard tapping at the door and ran out in expectation of Kip, who had promised to drop off mushrooms.

Lorraine stood there, made of pixels through the screen door. He, on the other hand, was barefoot and wearing only a pair of black shorts that had mysteriously shrunk.

She turned away, her face flushing. "I'm too early," she said. And then—as if she'd offended him, for it must have occurred to her that he might actually have planned to spend the night half naked—she stuttered, "Or I mean I haven't."

His hand worked by its own accord, luckily, and opened the door.

Something snapped behind him—like the sound of a log in a fire.

His vegetables weren't entirely burned except for one wayward circle of zucchini, singed uniformly black. She had followed him into the kitchen. He decided to pretend she was on time. He turned off the stove, asked her to excuse him for a second and promptly returned in a white shirt and long pants, both brutally wrinkled.

She was staring at the cod as if she didn't dare look elsewhere. He understood then. The stupid calendar that Kip gave him for his birthday was fluttering in the breeze from the screen door and sending the Portuguese woman's breasts into pneumatic ascent and sudden decline.

Lorraine helped him carry the plates and silverware out to the back porch where they ate at a small table. Gradually Jake began to relax, thanks to her sudden talkativeness. He wasn't paying too much attention to what she said, a pleasant hum about the food, about Ginny, about childhood summers in Gloucester, about an allergic reaction to strawberries. His former wife's presence didn't intervene except for a moment when he felt incredible relief at how lightly—in some ways—he'd been touched by that marriage after all, how grateful he was (in a manner only faintly tinged by resentment) that his wife put an end to it. He was aware of being mildly drunk without having downed his entire glass of wine. With delayed comprehension he recalled that Lorraine said she was allergic. The strawberries he'd hulled would have to disappear. As darkness settled over the porch he asked if she'd like to come inside. She said she shouldn't, and he understood. She asked for more wine.

At last when she did come inside there was a sound like gravel hurled at the windows followed by great splatterings of rain. He could hear the stone porch being pelted and then all at once a sound like buckets of water exploding. He felt instinctive dread, but when he reminded himself he wasn't on a boat but in the warmth of his home something in his chest expanded. His legs were turning soft. From where he sat with the rain only yards away and the sycamore's lower branches crazily swaying and the window turning white in the downpour he felt immensely fortunate.

Lorraine was oblivious to the storm, her back to the window. The sea would be wild—the island invisible to approaching boats, as if it were a secret out there, his own, somehow, illogical as that was—its black volcanic rock slippery, the white surge thrashing, the entire sky turning over.

14

That Kip and the new girl were missing wasn't understood immediately. The sailboat found its way back but not the couple. The girl's friend called the sheriff and the Coast Guard set out just as they had for Jake's little nun.

Jake was rushing to fill water jugs for his boat and his own search when Ervin Cu appeared outside the screen door—a hulking shadow even at his age.

"Come on in," Jake called out, bewildered. He had never spoken more than three sentences to Ervin Cu in his life, but with Kip missing Jake was both keyed up and detached from the moment. He watched his own hands under the water tap. They might as well belong to someone else.

Ervin Cu seemed to be walking toward him in slow motion. Jake was overcome by impatience. If no one so far had found Kip or the girl that didn't mean it was time to give up.

"I came over to say something and I'll say it now." Ervin's face was near purple.

"I don't have any time. You might have heard about Kip—."

"You can't do any good there. There's nowhere you'll look that they haven't already looked. So you're not in a hurry."

"I am."

"I came here to warn you."

Again a slowness in Cu—as if time were visible. Hairs bristled in red and black tufts from the craters of his face. An image came to Jake: a broken brick wall.

"You are to stay away from Marian."

Who's Marian? Jake nearly asked. Then he knew.

"I watched you follow her into St. Agatha's. I know you hold a grudge, but you can stop. You don't understand her and even if you did—."

Ervin Cu broke off, a flash of apprehension streaking his face.

Jake was heading to the door. Ervin followed him. As Jake ran down the walk he heard Ervin close the door behind him and rattle the knob to make sure the house was securely locked.

The Coast Guard, Jeff Dooley's boat—no luck. Jake headed out and took Owen Pasteur with him. They drew past Doug Llewellen's boat, filled with a pack of what looked like one hundred percent priests. Doug was in the cabin and had a kid working with him that Jake didn't recognize. "Kip's smart," Owen said. "A good swimmer. But the young lady—what about her?"

A seal glided off a rock island. Jake was reminded of his admiration for them. They belonged to two elements and were humble nevertheless.

Owen was mumbling. "Silly kid took her out—but she bewitched him."

"It's less complex than that, I think."

"You would think that."

"There's a chance they're holed up somewhere."

"What? You mean they faked it so he could get time with her?"

Jake didn't say that he wouldn't put it past the girl. Kip—he didn't think Kip would be involved in any game like that.

The sea was white grey by noon, but by three in the afternoon it was a faint blue, like a fading tattoo.

When Jake and Owen found Kip and the girl slogging about on the eastern shore of the island Jake wanted to shout and drop to his knees. The look on their faces stopped him. They were walking, the two of them, Kip trailing along behind the girl, with his head dropped, and the girl striding ahead, eyes small with anger.

"You're alive," Jake called out. He caught the flicker of something in Kip's eyes. Jake tried to wink at the girl—but his eyes, both, squinted. He couldn't help it. He threw his head back and laughed.

"I don't know," Owen said. "The young lady's alive. But Kip. Is that really Kip?"

Jake couldn't make himself stop laughing. "The new Kip," he said, at last.

"Except worse, man. From here he looks like he's in shock."

Jake shouted to Kip, "Where are my mushrooms?"

15

Three nuns were among the passengers on Tuesday. The nuns were older than his little nun and seemed nice enough, and eager to see the island. They were a relief given the three high-strung, stringily athletic academic couples who made up the remainder of passengers. Jake decided he would climb to the summit with this group and stick close to the nuns, the youngest of whom—maybe in her later thirties—sat on the second bench with her hands between her knees and laughed at Kip, who was sticking his chin up and his chest out in imitation of a stalwart sailor or something ridiculous.

Owen had been right about Kip. He wasn't the same Kip really. Manic maybe. The new manic Kip. Half the time he dashed around on deck like he was chased by bees. The other half of the time he was mugging, making worse jokes than usual. In some ways he had become the ideal tour guide to the island...if he could slow down part of the time. Jake would bet that Brittany would be back in the picture. But he recognized his bias; the other girl—her name, fittingly, turned out to be Celeste—was someone Jake couldn't help confining to a broad human category into which his former wife fit.

It was a disappointment to the academics in the group when, before ascending the summit, they trudged to the gift shop and found it locked and couldn't get into the tea room. One of the men hadn't had his morning coffee, and it showed. His wife seemed to think it was her business to reveal her support for her spouse by projecting an air of menace. Meanwhile the nuns were stamping their feet in the cold mist outside the chapel—also locked.

Jake knocked at the cottage. After he heard nothing inside he went to the window to the west, cupped his eyes, and leaned in. He heard a high voice—Ginny's?—on the other side of the wall. When the door was opened he looked down into the little girl's huge eyes. Past her he saw her father lying on the floor.

There was a bubble of blood on Carlo's temple where he must have caught the edge of the dinner table as he fell.

16

Maybe Ginny wanted the couch cushions to hide legions of plasticine horses and the bucketful of rubber snakes to be spilled permanently across the bathroom floor. Maybe the disorder was part of a plan, a regular feature of the cottage. Or had she hoped to scare Jake off on that first day he took over for her father while Carlo recuperated at Jake's house in Truror?

Jake dumped the snakes back in the bucket and allowed the two nail polish-decorated rubber turtles to continue clinging to the tub's rim. He repaired three steps leading to the summit, swept sand and pebbles out of the chapel, and withstood lame jokes from Kip and his new thick-faced buddy and crewmate Josh, both of whom were running the tour boat in Jake's absence. Josh's overly energetic performances as tour guide seemed to be draining Kip's. Which might not be such a bad thing.

The routine on the island was simple for Jake— opening the gift shop, cleaning out the unisex restroom and the tiny kitchen, putting out the coffee and tea canisters, setting out the hard biscuits, the non-dairy creamer and the sugar packets, unlocking the chapel and making sure the vigil candles hadn't burned a hole anywhere. The gift shop involved an adding machine and a cash box with a key. That left plenty of time for Jake to think his own thoughts and wander the island after Kip's or Doug Llewellyn's passengers left.

It was a different life for him—a waiting life. Carlo was doing reasonably well at the house in Truror, although he was warned that a side effect of radical heart surgery was depression. Lorraine had taken a leave of absence to help him and Ginny.

After the first week of caretaking, Jake had Carlo's canvases, paints, and brushes packed up and sent to him on the boat by way of Kip. In another box he stuffed more of Ginny's toys to be delivered to her. It was surprising how few personal belongings Carlo and his little girl owned. There was a closet of women's clothes: Carlo's wife's things. Upon the discovery, Jake shut the door as if he needed to be quiet about it.

Two weeks later Lorraine appeared, brought over by Kip, and carrying what looked like an overnight satchel. Carlo needed time with Ginny—alone, she said. Jake's tongue clamped to the roof of his mouth.

He had showered, shaved, the works, but he was primarily a big sweat gland. A sweat gland that made dinner. In the tiny bathroom he lifted up his shirt and clapped water under his arms and applied soap he found in a bowl. Only when he walked back into the dining room did he realize he smelled like lilacs.

Dinner began with a creamed tomato soup. He tried to like his own cooking but his gastric juices ruined his appetite. The soup tasted like it carried a whiff of vomit. The spindly kitchen chairs reminded him of something from an ice cream parlor. He had to be careful not to tip over. Only when Lorraine suddenly pressed his hand against her shirt did he relax. Even then, there was a dreaded half-second when he imagined she was having a heart attack.

The following Saturday, Jake was surprised to see Carlo and Ginny heading up the path. Kip lagged behind them and gave Jake a half-guilty, half-helpless look.

Carlo's legs at last stopped just outside the cottage, though the rest of him kept swaying. By the stubborn set of his jaw it was clear he meant for Jake to reclaim the house in Truror. The last thing Carlo wanted to do, it seemed, was to keep Jake out of his own home for any length of time.

Ginny carried a beach bag with dolls poking out of it. She was looking up at her father as if he might topple over.

After Jake was sure he couldn't convince Carlo to take it easy in Truror, he started to bargain.

"Okay. I'll head home and you're back in the cot-

tage. But I want to keep up the caretaker duties."
He added quickly, "During days. Just until you're a
little more ready to ease back into the job."

"I am ready."

"Well—I'll just keep on for a short stint then.
I'm in the habit. I almost know what I'm doing."

"I owe you a lot," Carlo said.

Ginny set her beach bag on the ground and
clasped her father's hand.

17

As soon as the news came to him by way of Mrs. Gustuf, it seemed wrong to stay at home but just as wrong to attend Marian Cu's funeral.

From his kitchen window Jake watched Ervin Cu drive off alone on the morning of the service.

At two o'clock Jake drove to St. Agatha's. The parking lot was filled and the sandstone church was silent but throbbed with some withheld energy—perhaps at any moment doors would fling open and everything before his eyes would come into fierce life. He parked across the street, keeping the car idling, and when the doors at last opened and he realized that the coffin was probably on its way through the south exit, he watched the mourners suck in air as if drowning.

Ervin Cu was being attended by a woman, her arm around his shoulder. It was Lorraine, her face stiff and old-looking while Cu was bent forward like the weight of his head was dragging him down to the ground.

Jake waited until the lot emptied and the last car snaked away behind the hearse.

When he got back home and Kip showed up, Jake sent him away, or thought he had. An hour later Jake heard scraping on the porch. Kip. Still there. Sitting on the steps.

By then Jake could talk. They sat in the kitchen—Kip silent, but Jake knowing he would talk eventually. What else would he have been waiting for?

"She was pretty disappointed," Kip said.

"Oh." Was he talking about Marian Cu or Lorraine?

"Really disappointed."

Kip must have meant the fox-faced girl—Celeste.

"Well, to hell with that," Jake said. "Want some eggs? Peggy Gustuf brought over some bacon she wanted out of the house."

"Why would she want bacon out of the house? Is it going bad? Does bacon even go bad?"

"Bacon can't be improved on."

"You know—Celeste is like someone from another planet. A planet not from our galaxy. Not even from a neighboring galaxy."

"Thank god you escaped with your faculties intact."

"Who said I have?"

"How'd you wind up on that side of the island?"

"Her idea—for drowning me. She thought she was a good swimmer."

"And she's not."

"Let's just say that synchronized swimming has not lost a champion in her."

"You're lucky she didn't drown you both."

"She tried…and then later she tried to make it up to me in a pretty weird way." Kip rested his head on the kitchen table. He mumbled into his elbow. "Oh man did I piss her off. I wasn't even trying. I've kind of graduated from Brittany, I guess. You can say," Kip raised his voice and laughed, "I'm a slave to passion."

"God help you."

Jake had heard that packages were going around. Only four days after the funeral he came home to find a sack on his porch. Inside, four albums. Photographs—his mother in many of them. He could have used those when he was a boy. Yellow cellophane sheets stuck to pictures of his mother— younger and younger in each album. Then very young. With another little girl that he determined, after some difficulty, to be Marian Cu. Two little girls, holding hands. Marian Cu leaning in. She had always loved his mother. Mrs. Cu, terrible cannibal that she was. He turned the pages, unwilling to stop for long even at one photo—his mother in her chair, his boyhood self in her lap, his left hand around her neck. His head was turned partly away. Even so, a sneer was visible, etched on that defiant little face. Mrs. Cu must have taken the photograph. For a moment he nearly understood Mrs.

Cu. He would be reluctant to like that child. He would have felt an instinctive reluctance to come closer to that knotted little muscle of fear disguised as rage.

He put the albums away in the room that had been his mother's. The albums smelled like Mrs. Cu. He was surprised that even the memory of her smell had lasted all these years. Had infected some part of his memory. He wished he pitied Marian Cu the way he pitied Ervin. Not that there was anything left to pity.

18

She was on his porch—where the surprises arrived lately.

Her hair was pulled back, and she was wearing a faded denim skirt, which made Jake recall uncomfortably the women who buried baby clothes at the island's summit. A moment of vertigo almost caught him before he was able to look squarely into Lorraine's eyes.

She was explaining that Mrs. Cu was her aunt—by her mother's second marriage and through Ervin.

She held out a square of paper. Paper folded many times over into a tiny thick packet perforated with holes. When Jake didn't unfold the paper but continued to stare she explained herself. She had found the packet behind the satin padding in a sewing basket. Ervin Cu had given the basket to her, along with other sewing supplies that used to belong to Marian. The satin backing in the basket was coming loose. It was not unheard of for the old baskets made in Japan to have newspapers used as linings, newspapers with interesting markings. Out of curiosity and to smooth out the backing Lorraine had drawn out the padding.

Before she left the cottage, she said, "I wouldn't have read it if I had known. Not even if I had guessed."

It was some time before Jake could get himself to look at what she'd left him.

The note was addressed to him. It was so short that he kept re-reading, as if more lines of handwriting might magically appear:

Don't ever doubt my love for you.
Mrs. Cu has made me a sacred promise.
She will take care of you better than I can.

As if the past was happening in front of him, the memory bulked, wavered, and rose. He could see again everything around his mother. Magnified. Clarified. The oil seacape on the wall above her head flew toward him with its bright slashes of blue, the schooner's ivory sails billowing, and a smaller schooner sailing behind it, like a miniaturized mirror image. Golden-brown light searched about in the room. The light from the kitchen was on and beaming from around the corner. A window was open and the wind and the light from the window played with shadows. Mrs. Cu sat at the side of his mother, like a royal attendant, a lady

19

The sight of what looked like a rolled-up rug caught in a seaweed island attracted the attention of three boys setting out on their sailboat before the storm broke. The fabric, huge, twisted, was like a shroud, as if the body was sewn into the thing for burial. The boys pushed the body to shore.

What was left had to be unwound. Still in heavy shoes, the body. No identification was found, and no one claimed the body. The coroner determined the corpse to be male and dressed, apparently, in a monk's garb.

20

In less than two months the tour boats wouldn't be running. "Maybe by then my heart can be trusted," Carlo told Jake, though soon thereafter he suffered another setback, a scare more than anything but serious enough to get his attention. He had to settle once more at Jake's house in Truror. Lorraine again took time off from the library to care for him and look after Ginny, and to make sure he didn't rush things a second time.

But Lorraine needn't have worried. It occurred to Jake on a late August afternoon that he wanted to remain the island's caretaker, that he was knotted into the fabric of the place.

Below him, sea hawks glided, skimming over invisible panes of glass. He stood at the top of the highest cliff behind the chapel. It had become a ritual with him, at the close of any day, to watch the clouds fold over the mainland in the distance, settling on Truror. Slowly, he began to feel a presence behind him, nearly at his heel. When a hand touched his shoulder he didn't draw back. He let his legs fold under him until he was sitting, as did the woman he had thought of as his nun, her robe tucked under her knees.

The wind rose, catching at the nun's veil, whipping it across Jake's face. He didn't lift his hands to push away the cloth from his eyes. What he saw through the veil: everything shot through with silver threads of light. The nun batted it back for him. They sat in silence together. Gradually, ahead of them, Jake could see scores of women and men. They were crowding the edge of the cliff. There were women in dresses and nightgowns twisting in the wind, women in half-habits and thick shoes, women in long pants, men in jackets, men in long robes, too. They were dropping from sight, over the cliff. A woman in a skirt kicked off into air. For an instant she looked stuck halfway, as if her legs disappeared in a pocket between worlds. And then he saw, tucked close against her chest: a newborn, it looked like, enveloped in a little pink jacket that the baby hadn't had time to grow into.

The nun pulled at his arm. He imagined she would guide him, and the two of them would take a few steps forward to join the assembly falling through the air.

His nun drew his head down. She began speaking, close to his ear. "They look disappointed—some of them," she said. "It's hard for them. They've wanted to return so badly. I've led them this far but no farther."

He was a man used to belittling his own thoughts, but he did not belittle his vision of the spirits stopping off on the island, making the tour of all they thought they'd renounced: the smell of thin soil, the warmth of the sun on rocks, the ocean, gleaming and sliding, and giving up eventually its sunken travelers.

He wanted to ask about his mother and felt a chill at the thought. She would not be among the saints. Nor would she have wanted to return. His little nun craned forward, her gaze fixed on a tall man poised on a rock at the edge of the cliff. Jake was sure that his nun wanted to see, the moment he turned to her, the changing lights in that man's face.

Jake would not forget her, but neither would he be thinking of the nun when he took the skiff to Truror, determined to see Carlo and Ginny in the home that he was going to be giving up to them—and to see Lorraine, if he could, if she let him, given that he hadn't made any effort with her after she brought him the note. Hardly forgivable of him. When he was back on land, the sidewalk gave off a smell like a hot frying pan dropped into cold water. Any instant, there'd be rain. In the distance new clouds sped across the island. Already, anyone approaching from the water might watch the island come to life and fly. As he walked, he was aware of the sound of the ocean, the steady sway of it—a relentless miracle. The rain dashing across his face felt warm and alive.

Acknowledgments

I want to express my deep gratitude to Joseph Bates for his editing of this novella. How lucky I have been to have had the benefit of his remarkable insight. I remain very grateful to Lafayette College and my colleagues there for continued support of my work. As always, my independent-minded sisters and my miraculous mother are inspirations to me. I write with memories of both my father and my brother close to my heart. Finally, I could not be more fortunate in my husband Eric Ziolkowski and our daughters, Theodora and Cecilia. Whenever I've needed a guide, those three have led me.

Biographical Note

Theodora Ziolkowski

Lee Upton is the author of five books of poetry, most recently *Undid in the Land of Undone*, and four books of literary criticism. She is the recipient of a Pushcart Prize, the National Poetry Series Award, and awards from the Poetry Society of America. Her fiction has appeared in *The Antioch Review*, *Epoch*, *Shenandoah*, and other journals.

Other titles from Miami University Press

Poetry

The Bridge of Sighs, Steve Orlen
People Live, They Have Lives, Hugh Seidman
This Perfect Life, Kate Knapp Johnson
The Dirt, Nance Van Winckel
Moon Go Away, I Don't Love You No More, Jim Simmerman
Selected Poems: 1965–1995, Hugh Seidman
Neither World, Ralph Angel
Now, Judith Baumel
Long Distance, Aleda Shirley
What Wind Will Do, Debra Bruce
Kisses, Steve Orlen
Brilliant Windows, Larry Kramer
After A Spell, Nance Van Winckel
Kingdom Come, Jim Simmerman
Dark Summer, Molly Bendall
The Disappearing Town, John Drury
Wind Somewhere, and Shade, Kate Knapp Johnson
The Printer's Error, Aaron Fogel
Gender Studies, Jeffrey Skinner
Ariadne's Island, Molly Bendall
Burning the Aspern Papers, John Drury
Beside Ourselves, Nance Van Winckel
Rainbow Darkness: an anthology of African-American poetry,
Keith Tuma, Ed.
Talk Poetry, Mairéad Byrne
Between Cup and Lip, Peter Manson
Virgil's Cow, Frederick Farryl Goodwin

Fiction

Edited by the Creative Writing Faculty of Miami University
Mayor of the Roses, Marianne Villanueva
The Waiting Room, Albert Sgambati
Badlands, Cynthia Reeves
A Fight in the Doctor's Office, Cary Holladay

Nonfiction

*Performing Worlds into Being: Native American
Women's Theater,* A. E. Armstrong, K. L.
Johnson, W. A. Wortman, Eds.